After
HAPPILY
—EVER—
AFTER

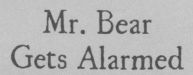

Mr. Bear
Gets Alarmed

...er Happily Ever After is published by Stone Arch Books
...Capstone Imprint
710 Roe Crest Drive
North Mankato, Minnesota 56003
www.capstonepub.com

First published by Orchard Books, a division of Hachette Children's Books
338 Euston Road, London NW1 3BH, United Kingdom

Library of Congress Cataloging-in-Publication Data is available
on the Library of Congress website.

ISBN-13: 978-1-4342-7948-4 (hardcover)
ISBN-13: 978-1-4342-7954-5 (paperback)

Summary: After the Goldilocks break-in, Mr. Bear is extra anxious. He
installs a state-of-the-art alarm system and insists that Mrs. Bear and Baby
Bear use it at all times. But it soon gets to be too much when he starts
worrying about what might happen to his family outside the home, too.
Can Mrs. Bear help Mr. Bear realize that he can't control everything?

Designer: Russell Griesmer
Photo Credits: ShutterStock/Maaike Boot, 4, 5, 55

Printed in China.
092013   007737LEOS14

After HAPPILY —EVER— AFTER

Mr. Bear
Gets Alarmed

by TONY BRADMAN
illustrated by SARAH WARBURTON

STONE ARCH BOOKS®
a capstone imprint

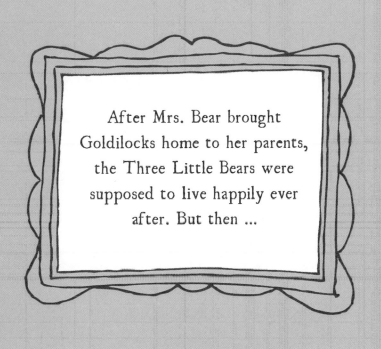

After Mrs. Bear brought
Goldilocks home to her parents,
the Three Little Bears were
supposed to live happily ever
after. But then ...

"You're in a funny mood," said Mrs. Bear, turning to her husband. "I hope you're not still brooding about what happened last week. You need to get over it, dear."

The Three Bears had just eaten a
delicious supper in their little cottage. Now
Mr. and Mrs. Bear were doing the dishes
while Baby Bear watched TV.

"Brooding? Me? Certainly not!" said Mr.
Bear. "But I have been doing some thinking.
I've decided we should get a burglar alarm."

"Isn't that a bit extreme?" said Mrs. Bear, frowning. "Goldilocks won't do it again, I'm sure of it."

"Maybe she won't," said Mr. Bear. "But if a young girl can break in, then anybody can. And the forest is full of dangerous characters these days. You've seen the scary stories on the news."

The truth was that Mr. Bear had been very rattled by the whole Goldilocks incident.

He hadn't slept well since then. He woke up several times each night, convinced he could hear a window being opened or footsteps on the stairs.

The only way to stop worrying was to get an alarm system, and the sooner the better.

"I don't take as much notice of the news stories as you do," said Mrs. Bear, shrugging. "But you can have an alarm if it will make you happy. Now, how about a cup of tea?"

But Mr. Bear's cup of tea went cold. He
sat in front of his computer, searching the
Forest Web for companies that installed
alarms. He hadn't realized there were so
many! And the alarm systems they sold
were so complicated.

"You could try any of them," said Mrs. Bear. "They all look the same to me."

"But they're not," murmured Mr. Bear. "What if I choose one that's not good?"

"Fine, you carry on," said Mrs. Bear. "I'll put Baby Bear to bed on my own."

Mr. Bear finally made his choice hours later, long after Baby Bear and Mrs. Bear had gone to bed. And the sun had barely risen the next morning when the man from Wizard Security rang the doorbell.

Soon he was scattering cables and
wires everywhere. Mrs. Bear was still
in her nightgown, and not very happy
about being disturbed so early.

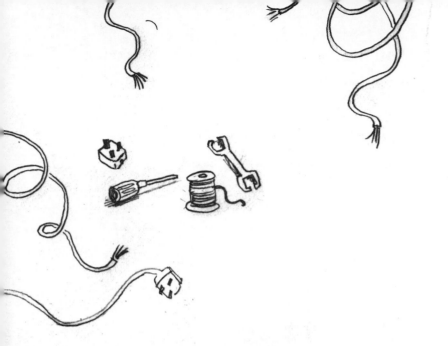

"There you go," said the man at last.
He was in the hall, screwing a small box
to the wall.

"You just need to think of a secret code, then you're all set. You tap it into this keypad to turn the system on and off."

"Great, thanks!" said Mr. Bear, as the man waved goodbye.

Mr. Bear turned to his wife. "Now, let's think of a code. We should make it really hard to guess."

"I'll leave that up to you, dear," sighed Mrs. Bear. "I have to get ready."

Mr. Bear always gave Mrs. Bear a ride to work, then dropped Baby Bear off at school. He wrote down the code he had made up and gave it to them.

They were supposed to memorize it, then destroy the pieces of paper.

Mr. Bear drove home in the sunshine, feeling happy and relaxed for the first time in ages.

He tapped in the code to turn off the alarm, then cleared away the breakfast dishes.

He made the beds and did some ironing,
which was one of his favorite chores.

That night he slept really well.

Life went by peacefully, and on Saturday
they went shopping to buy Baby Bear
some school shoes. Back at home, Mr. Bear
was locking the car when he gasped in
horror at his wife.

Mrs. Bear was reading their secret code from a piece of paper!

"What are you doing?" said Mr. Bear. "You were supposed to destroy that!"

"Well, you made the code too hard to remember, so I didn't," said Mrs. Bear. "I don't see what the big deal is, anyway. I keep it in my purse."

"But what if someone steals your purse?" squeaked Mr. Bear.

"No problem," Baby Bear piped up. "I've written the code on my paw."

"Oh no!" groaned Mr. Bear. "What if someone has seen it already? We'll have to change it. Maybe we should have a different code every week, or even for every day."

Mrs. Bear and Baby Bear rolled their
eyes, but Mr. Bear made them promise they
would memorize the new code.

But soon Mr. Bear decided that it still
wasn't enough. So he called Wizard Security
once more.

"There you go," said the man. "Now you have the best system money can buy. Separate alarms in each room ...

cameras inside the cottage ...

and in the garden ...

and a panic button that connects you directly to the Forest Police."

Mr. Bear relaxed again. But that night, just after the bears had gone to bed, there was a terrible noise. All the alarms had gone off at once!

DANG-A-LANG-A-LANG!

Mrs. Bear grabbed Baby Bear, Mr. Bear ran around yelling, and the Forest Police arrived, lights flashing and sirens wailing.

WHOOP-WHOOP-WHOOP!

"You can calm down now, Mr. Bear," said a policeman, once the alarms had stopped. "We're pretty sure no one was trying to break in. These complicated alarm systems can sometimes be too sensitive. A squirrel might have set it off, or even a mouse."

"Oh, terrific," muttered Mrs. Bear. Then she took Baby Bear back to bed.

After that, the bears were very careful at night. But hardly a day went by without one of the alarms going off, and sometimes all of them at once.

The bears got to know the Forest Police very well.

Then one day, much to Mr. Bear's surprise, the alarms didn't go off. They didn't go off the next day, either. Mr. Bear was very pleased.

"You see?" he said, grinning. "I knew they would settle down eventually."

"Of course you did, dear," said Mrs. Bear. For some reason, Baby Bear giggled, and Mrs. Bear frowned at him. "Now, would you like some tea before bed?"

A happy and relaxed Mr. Bear went to bed that evening.

Mr. Bear fell into a deep, dreamless sleep, but suddenly he was awake. His heart was pounding.

He could hear footsteps on the stairs, and he couldn't hear any alarms!

Mr. Bear crept out of the bedroom and onto the landing. He looked down, and there was Mrs. Bear in the hall, tapping a code into the keypad.

She glanced up at him, and a guilty
expression passed over her face. Then
she scowled.

"All right, you caught me," she said, and
sighed. "We've been turning the alarms off
every night. We just couldn't cope with it
anymore."

"Oh no! What if someone had broken in?" moaned Mr. Bear. "What if …"

"They didn't though, did they?" said Mrs. Bear. "And what if you're just worrying too much? What if your alarms are making our lives a misery?"

Mr. Bear realized Mrs. Bear was right.
Now it was his turn to feel guilty.

The alarms certainly hadn't stopped him from worrying, had they? In fact they had only made things much worse.

Mr. Bear did a lot of thinking that day, and finally he came to a decision.

He called Wizard Security for the last time, and it wasn't long before all the alarms were gone.

The next morning, Mr. Bear woke up in a cheerful mood.

"What a lovely day!" he said. "Let's go for a walk."

They set off on their usual path through the Forest. Baby Bear skipped ahead of his parents. Suddenly, Mrs. Bear stopped and looked at her husband.

"Oh no, I forgot to lock the front door!"
she said. "We better go back!"

Mr. Bear turned to her, and for an instant he felt a little panicky. But then he smiled, shrugged, and took her arm.

"Not to worry," he said as they walked on. "I'm sure it will be all right."

And so the Three Bears lived quietly
and calmly and most of all HAPPILY EVER
AFTER!

ABOUT THE AUTHOR

Tony Bradman writes for children of all ages. He is particularly well known for his top-selling Dilly the Dinosaur series. His other titles include the Happily Ever After series, *The Orchard Book of Heroes and Villains*, and *The Orchard Book of Swords*, *Sorcerers*, and *Superheroes*. Tony lives in South East London.

ABOUT THE ILLUSTRATOR

Sarah Warburton is a rising star in children's books. She is the illustrator of the Rumblewick series, which has been very well received at an international level. The series spans across both picture books and fiction. She has also illustrated nonfiction titles and the Happily Ever After series. She lives in Bristol, England, with her young baby and husband.

GLOSSARY

brooding (BROOD-ing) — worrying or thinking about something

convinced (kuhn-VINSST) — made a person believe you

cope (KOPE) — to deal with something in a positive way

installed (in-STAWLD) — put something in place

murmured (MUR-murd) — talked quietly

rattled (RAT-uhld) — upset or embarrassed

scowled (SKOULD) — made an angry frown

sensitive (SEN-suh-tiv) — reacts easily to a small change

shrugging (SHRUHG-ing) — raising your shoulders to show doubt or lack of interest

DISCUSSION QUESTIONS

1. Do you think this story was a good addition to the original story of Goldilocks and the Three Bears? Why or why not?

2. Do you think Mr. Bear went overboard with the alarm system? Explain your answer.

3. What would you use as a code for an alarm system? Why?

WRITING PROMPTS

1. Pretend you are Mrs. Bear. Write a journal entry about how you feel about the new alarm system.

2. Did you know Mrs. Bear was turning off the alarm system? Look back in the story and write down any clues you can find.

3. Make a list of at least three things Mr. Bear could have done instead of installing the alarm system.

THE FUN DOESN'T STOP HERE!